Pearls
of my heart

Poems by

VITALE

With love,

for Kitch

Table of Contents

Introduction

*T*he waves gently lapped against the side of the dock under the moonlight as a Polish woman approached the gangplank of the dominating naval vessel. Onboard was her husband, U.S. Lieutenant John Christy. Despite the wintery whispers, the woman's palms were sweating, and her heart raced as she weighed the gravity of the decision on her mind. If she continued forward, she knew she would never see her homeland or any of her remaining kinsmen ever again. She would be stowing away and illegally entering the United States. If she turned around and returned to the city, she would be at the mercy of a political force that inserted itself into her country's anxious power vacuum. The war had taken most of her family, so what protection against communism could she have with a husband stationed thousands of miles across the sea? Like most things during those days, the bureaucratic red tape was in the way, and the process of her citizenship would have taken a year (hopefully). This was her husband's last night in Poland before shipping off, and she was warned earlier by a close friend that it would be her last chance to escape. She was damned either way.

I never had the opportunity to meet my grandfather, but my grandmother told me that he was a strong, stoic, disciplined man and that she loved him very much. Was that why she took the risk of a lifetime and (against the wishes of her husband) got on the ship that cold night in the heart of the 1940's? Maybe the call of a higher power whispered into her ear to board. Perhaps it was the fear of the unknown, post-liberation. What I do know is that her defiant act of love cascaded into a series of events that will continue to culminate long after I am also gone and that no matter how grim the situations are, God will continue to reveal His plan in His favorite form of communication, love.

The following collection is not about my grandparents. However, it would be the collection I would share with my grandparents to relay my feelings about love, most specifically, the woman I fell in love with. While the circumstances of my love story are a far stretch (and then some) from that of my grandparents, their story has me aghast at the juxtaposition of the modern dating world adjacent to that of their own. Our grandparents' environment gave them every reason not to fall in love, yet even in the heart of the world's greatest conflict, men and women couldn't help but give into their most crucial and basic instincts. They were not afraid to take big risks in the name of love, and at least in the case of my grandparents, they were rewarded for their courage. Since then, dating customs have shifted drastically. The United States is facing a potential demographic collapse because young people aren't taking risks, falling in love, and settling down in stable marriages at the same rates that we are used to when our grandparents walked through and collected the broken pieces of nihilistic rubble. Yet, modern movements such as "bolting" and the current waves of feminism have men and women at odds, and young people feel lonelier than ever. Such groups could argue their differences till the morning cock crows, but one commonality that cannot be avoided is understanding, affection, and love.

Love is an uncontrollable force. You cannot catch it, touch it, buy it, or summon it, but you can recognize it; You can feel and see love. You can even be inspired to build or bulldoze a kingdom because of it. You can give it to them. Love is the greatest known unknown of mankind and it kind of works a little like lightning. You never know when or where it's going to strike, but once it does, its effects are violently electrifying. I was struck by the mysterious force we call love, and as a result, I wrote the following collection of poems. I hope they reassure and inspire those who feel like they've been waiting forever for "the one" to finally come along. Be patient, my friends, and take the current moment to lean into the virtues offered by our Lord. You have a lot of power because of your free will but know that God has a plan for you, and part of that plan probably includes meeting someone who will absolutely shatter your expectations for a potential mate. I didn't think it could ever happen to me, but I was wrong. I thank God every day that I was wrong about love.

Until Forever

My life was not meant for this world.
My life is as valuable as swirling dust
Kicked up by the Lord
And breathed upon by an immortal wind,
A sharp wind that I've been running against.
With each step, an additional particle is stripped
From me and returned to my master.
Soon, I will disintegrate,
Disapparate into the whisper of the breeze.
All parts will return to the ground
To be trampled underfoot,
Save two particles of dust.
One for you to carry in your heart,
And one for God to carry me home.
Mourn me not when I evaporate from this world.
But allow the speck of dust
To invigorate your belief that one day
You and I shall meet again
In a place overwhelming with love.
Our souls were bound together on this earth
Our souls will find each other beyond
An eternal comfort and rest
In the heart of our Savior
At the center of God's eye.

Ghost

That was pretty fast,
You vanished in a flash,
The moment didn't last.
Ended in a crash.

Is this how you feel?
Because I just don't know.
Are you even real?
No. No.

You're just a ghost.
Vapor and air.
You never existed.
There is nothing there.
Spin the wheel again
Or just close the door.
No more. Know more.

You sparked so brightly.
Was it just a lie?
Smitten from the start
Why did the feeling die?

Well, I hope you're happy
And find him someday.
He's romantic and sappy
And only one swipe away.
No. No.

You're just a ghost.
Vapor and air.
You never existed.
There is nothing there.
Spin the wheel again,
Or just close the door.
No more. Know more.

Although I'm alone,
I'll quiet my heart.
It's a hidden gemstone,
A priceless work of art.
Then you came into my life
When the world seemed gray.
And now you're my wife
And I'm proud to say,

I love you the most.
More than vapor or air.
I thank God you exist,
And will always be there.
You're my only "again".
You're my open door.
Each day, I love you
Each day, even more.

Teach Me to Swim

We're sitting in a leaking boat,
But I believe we'll make it float.
We're in a vessel lost at sea.
Young, wild, and carefree.
On a journey with no map,
Through every blessing and mishap.

Two ships in the night meant only to pass.
We docked together and made the moment last.
We churned waves to tsunamis till dawn.
Down the whirlpool of a new phenomenon.

We're sitting in a leaking boat.
But I think we'll make it float.
A ship in the bottle lost at sea,
Discovering where we're meant to be.
A new adventure with no map,
Through every blessing and mishap.

Our anchors tangled beneath the surface.
Our heading aimed towards a higher purpose.
We pulled pearls from our archipelago,
Expanded and basked in a golden glow.

We're sitting in a leaking boat.
But I'm convinced we'll make it float.
A ship in the bottle shattered at sea,
Surrendering to God's responsibility.
Although our ship has turned to scrap,
We'll charge together through this mishap.

The winter splintered our sails.
The rain turned into hail,
But we vowed we would be true.
We'll hunt for the holy grail,
Come hell, high water, win or fail,
Because my heart belongs to you.

We're sitting in a holy boat
And I trust God to make it float.
We're in a vessel found at sea,
Sailing towards eternity.
On a journey hand in hand
Together, sailing towards God's plan.

Called to Love

Damn this pride
Buried in my soul.
Its roots run deep
And have total control.
It blossomed into a willow
That weeps all day.
Crying in the wind
If things don't go my way.

Sometimes I go too deep,
Spending time in the dark.
Navigating the pits
Of a sick human heart.
Because in the end
God's light will shine
And illuminate the good
Within all of mankind.

I don't believe
I'm a good man of faith.
I smoke too much weed
And get caught up in wrath.
Cause the pain is too much.
I'd rather be numb.
I don't care if I die,
Or if tomorrow will come.

I'm hanging by a thread
Not thinking before it's been said.
God, forgive the path I've tread.
God, get me out of my own head.
Countless tears, still to be shed.
Countless drops, still to be bled.
One more heart, still left to shred.
One more night, alone in my bed.

The light is coming.
Gold threads peeking over the edge.
A warmer new day is rising
Pulling me back from the ledge.
God granted my prayer,
A gift I don't deserve.
She's a sacred fire to tend to,
A holy vessel I must preserve.

Maybe I was wrong about it all,
A stubborn fool in the dark.
I've been blinded by the light
And her voice calls like a skylark.
An overwhelming harmonious coo
Guides my mind and my heart.
She sings a seductively sweet song,
Where I'm called to play my part.

A second chance,
A budding romance,
A blending of souls,
Creating something whole.
Damn this pride,
Cast it away.
Sever the roots
And start a new day.

Sanctuary

Lay down and be my holy resting place,
And let me lay my head upon your breast
As your breathing restores the grace in my mind.
I'm reminded of how blessed I am
As I run my fingers across your face.
Soft and delicate to the touch, and the spark
In your eye has possessed the thump of my
Heart. Moving steady, keeping a pittered pace
With the fountain of life within your chest.
You undulate gently like waves lapping
Like the universal cosmic ripples
Across space. Under the weight of your love,
I burrow into comfort and repose.

Found

What a wonderful series of footnotes.
Tiny blips of slow, deliberate Morse code
Ticking infrequently across hundreds
Of thousands of years, desperate
Communication longing to be understood.
A wheel turning, grinding itself down—
Racing itself against a trillion crystallized moments
Passing through a needle in the glass,
Creating a sharper, finely tuned curve.
Who won this race? Or are we just moving in circles
Across the event horizon of imagination?
Where everything exists everywhere all of the time,
but you are not an ever-expanding theorized
Figment. You are exactly and tethered
Where you're meant to be. Now, next to me,
Your heart combusts in harmony with the spark
Of divinity exploding ripples into the universe.
It echoes the cosmic collapse of stars eons away,
Scattering trillions upon trillions of particles
To be reborn in a desolate, unfertilized fathom of space.
Perhaps the stars do align to scroll our names
Across the void. When I gaze up into the speckled well
Of unknown distance, possibility, and power,
The only name I see written is yours.

Dance with Me

Our passions flare like two comets
Chasing each other across the cosmic void
Locked in the same fated loop, winding
And weaving a lasso traversing the sky.
Together, we summon a unique love story,
Following our fated path.
We're like two dancers,
Scrolling a timeless romance across the floor
In a language only they initiated can decipher.
The steps are learned, but the spontaneity shines.
An undistinguished hierarchy in a trusting connection.
The footwork bookends, but the passion embers
Between.
A similar ember that glows in our trail
As we sprint faster than bolts of lightning
Across the tundra vacuum of the universe,
Desperate to catch up with the other.
Someday, we shall collide and create
A fantastic light, exposing the particles
Of abandoned life hidden in folds of space.

Careless Summer

We ran to the meadow to pick sunflowers
On the longest, hottest summer day.
The grass was like delicate feathers,
That tickled our disposition as we rested.
You used my chest as a pillow
And clutched onto your wild bouquet
As if the slightest of breezes
Would swoop them into the air,
Like a cage of doves released
During the champagne of a wedding.

Our spirits evaporated under the heat
And danced like two playful lights,
Translucent only to the lover's eye.
Our eyes faded, closed, and we napped
Peacefully. Not a care in the world
As the wind gently kissed our skin.
What use is it to witness our spirits dance?
The sparks of our divinity collided
And ignited a fire so powerfully optimistic,
Like a new star being born out of the ether,
It caught the attention and smile of the Lord.

Looking Forward

I thought I was meant to sail the seas.
A lone mariner blistering his hands
Against a tightening sheet, fighting
A relentlessly shouting wind, in search
Of a cup of water to wet my tongue,
In search of an oasis to finally sleep.

But your gaze caught my attention,
And I dove headfirst into the thicket
Of forest in your eyes. I still mar my hands
For survival in these woods. I ally
With the wind to fuel my fire,
And gather rainwater to wet my tongue.

I peel back layers of bark
To better understand the sturdiness
Of the timber and count the number of rings
Wrapped around the center of your soul.
I embrace the Lord's commission, and vow
To keep vigilant stewardship over these woods.

Before I met you, I was drowning in the wind.
I was a broken cork aimlessly bobbing at the mercy
Of the sea. But purpose lies on the other side
Of your almond brown eyes. I plant a post
In the ground and root my claim to your heart.
I enter these woods and thank God I am lost.

Looking Back

The stem has extracted the last beads
Of sugar-coated water from the mineral root,
And the golden pages surrender their stories
To the mercy of the wind. A cyclical scattering
Tale of bucks that lock horns for the blush
Of the does. The final kiss of summer infused
These pages with hints of honeysuckle and lavender.
A delicious flavor has grown bitter to the taste.
The paper grew frail, crumpled, was trampled,
Left to be torn. Left to grow slimy and dirt-stained
After the monsoon season. Left to the forgetful
Memory of the silent trees. Soon, it will flurry.
And those without a campfire to huddle around
Are left to wonder what makes a louder sound:
The love story as it first hits the ground
Or the jagged, sharp flakes of frozen water
That bury it under a fresh canvas?

Surrender

She cried in my arms the night she surrendered
Her heart to my care. Tears that taste
Like fresh rainwater that catch and drip
Off perky emerald foliage. This nourishment
Leaks out of her reprimanded soul,
And spills into my cup, precious as liquid gold.

Each drop contains overwhelming joy
She was convinced would remain hidden
In the darkest crevices of her empathy.
A joy she believed was shameful and ugly.
She could not keep the vault door to her feelings
Barred any longer. A wonderful release.

A chance to trust again. Laugh again. Love again.
I lifted the cup to my unworthy lips
As if it were the elixir of immortality
And consumed the avalanche of her emotions.
The taste transubstantiated the trajectory of my life.
I am ready to drown upon the fearful desires of her heart.

Fire

Starting the fire was easy,
Maintaining the burn is hard.
Times are tough, money tight,
Resources to fuel the spark are scarce.
I'd comb the desolate landscape and steal
Any kindling to feed the insatiable embers,
And burn the shirt off my back
Just to keep you warm a little longer.
Especially on nights like this
When the breath of God's chill
Cuts straight through to the bone.
Even if we're stripped of everything,
We'll hold each other naked in the snow
Shivering next to the quickly fading coals.
Eventually, our steady beating hearts
Will be our only source of warmth.
When that time comes, I'll whisper in your ear,
"I promise it won't be long till morning."

The Fall of Troy

Helen gazed into the eyes of Achilles
As the light of his spirit faded. The blood
Pooled at his feet, and he relinquished
The last of his strength to her arms
Like a wounded lion, fighting for the honor
Of his pride. The once-strong lungs
No longer billowed to bursting and Helen
Wept as Achilles' breathing slowed.

"All of this. Everything. Was for you,"
He softly whispered. His resilient, unsullied
Face entranced Helen. Not a single line
For her to draw her fingertip across.
Although he wilted, her covetous love
For him never died. But preserved
A splintering moment of captured time
In her heart and enslaved her expectations.

"I did not long to burn cities to the ground,
And I did not choose to sail across the sea
Searching to enslave myself to expectation.
I chose to plant my love into the ground
Like a tree and watch it grow, and nurture
It together with you as the lines
On your face came to happier fruition.
I eschewed glory and chased the divine
Freedom at the center of your arched eyes."

Illusion

Some will watch us and call our affection
A magic trick. A deceptive affair meant to fool
Everyone. I entered your life slicker
Than a sleight of hand. A hidden ace that slipped
Out of your sleeve, granting claim over the river.
They will try to convince even you and I
That our act is a fraud. That wires hold us up
When we walk hand in hand across the air.
Their misapprehension is a projection
Of the plumes within their own crystal ball.
We look into the hazy smoke and see
Each other's faces reflected clearly.
You and I know the truth, nothing was hidden,
Nothing disappeared. No preplanning,
No shady backroom deals. There is no prestige.
You once told me that our love made you believe
In magic again. To me, our love made me believe
In God's blessing, mercy, and forever again.

An Offering

The wind was strong the day the diver
Rowed out to sea. He fought the rough tide
And made his way to a hidden tidal inlet
Where schools of fish dredged their way
Along the vast coral reef to their classroom.
The young fisherman anchored in a calm
Spot of clear water and lustfully gazed
At the Pinctada maxima, half buried in the sandy
Floor to keep cool. The man donned gloves
Made from the hide of an ox and tied
A large rock to his feet. He slung a sash across
His shoulder and splashed. To the depths, he sank.
He clunked on the floor and rummaged
Covetously for the oysters. The seconds felt like hours
And the man labored quickly, racing against
The strain within his lungs, desperate for fresh oxygen.
At the last moment, he rose, and broke the surface
Choking on new life, careful not to drop his trove.
With no time to rest, the hunter unsheathed a knife
And began prying the mollusks like a thief breaking
Into a locked bank vault. His hoard yielded nothing,
So back into the water he went and refilled his satchel.
Again, he surfaced and scraped through the shells.
Again, nothing. He repeated this process over and over
As the sun drew a long scorching streak across the sky.
The day grew short and yet, the diver continued
His vigil for uncracked shells. His strength
Was zapped and he nearly gave up all hope.

But his patience was not spent in vain.
On his last dive, the hunter pulled up a dented
Oyster and extracted a black pearl that shined
The man's reflection against the rays of the setting sun.
The fisherman pulled his wife's embroidered
Silk handkerchief from his pocket and wrapped
The layers of smooth nacre for safekeeping.
The hunter hoisted his weighing rock
And his anchor and began rowing home
To surprise his wife with a simple gift.

Still New

She sent me to the attic
To fetch the Christmas décor,
And I stumbled upon a trunk
Filled with memories of old.
Pictures of us when we jumped
Just a little higher to climb
To the tops of the trees.
The world was our backdrop,
Our faces uncorrupted
By the lashings of time,
And our hair without pepper,
Still thick and dark as the night.
Our search for unique sceneries
Has faded like the coloring
Of these photos. Our bodies
Have yielded to disorganization,
Like the contents of this attic.
But some details have never
Conceded to time, like the almond
Glint of brown in your eyes
Or the dimple at the corner
Of your smile. Some things remain
As new as when we first met.
When the moment was captured.

Some particulars are ageless,
Unlike us. Unlike these photos,
Some nuances are as precious
As a lamb gently sleeping on the hay.
Some things are meant to last
Forever.

Waking Up

I love seeing the sunlight
Drenched upon your face
Every day when we wake up.
The soft coo in your voice sings
As you say, "Good morning, my love."
You stretch out like a cat
Curving into a deep arch,
And tie yourself into a bow around me,
Gripping your claws into my back.
You press your cheek against my face
And bury me in a veil of thick hair,
Black as the darkest night.
We tangle in the sheets
As we toss and turn,
Engaged in a battle of kisses,
Attacking the field of each other's skin.
The profound joy in your smile
Outshines the halos of the seraphim
And your rippling laugh rings out
Like church bells calling sinners to Mass.
Although this moment is timeless to us,
We both know our fate is inescapable,
And the responsibilities of the day
Call us from the comfort of bed.
Rise we must, and rise we do,
Renewed to take on the day.
And reassured that when we return,
We'll pick back up where we left off.

Cyclical Change

My father once told me that
A woman changes with the seasons,
And you must study her over
The course of the world's rotation.

She will want to dance naked
During a midsummer thunderstorm.
She'll slip across the damp grass,
And twirl under the refreshing drops.

As the leaves lose their luster,
She'll gather the yearly fruits
Of your labor in preparation
For hibernation. For desolation.

Nothing remains but blankets of bitterly
Cold canvas across the horizon.
You must press her close at night,
And mar your hands gathering more wood.

Tend to the earth, and remove every rock,
Branch, and weed from your garden.
Every seed must be planted
Before the ground fully thaws.

My father once told me that a woman
Changes with the seasons, but if you care
For her, like a good man tends his garden,
The reward will be a life full of love.

An Invitation

Take my hand, and let's fall down
The rabbit hole of our imagination
Again, and together, we'll create white sand
Beaches, plush jungled volcano mountains,
And turquoise blue singing waterfalls.

Bathe with me in the whirlpool
Of your mind. The waters are clear,
Cool, and the floor is speckled
With gemstones of untapped wisdom.

Let me drink the nectar of your desires,
Quenching my starvation to know you.
I want to fly across the galaxy of your dreams,
Pocketing the stardust of your subconscious.
I long to vanquish the dragon in your nightmares,
And carry you off into our happily ever after.

Whether our fence be barbed wire or picket white,
Our China encrusted gold or contorted aluminum,
Our ground unproven fertile soil or barren rocky dust,
Nothing will snuff the eternal fire within our hearts.

Prayer

I thank God every day that she came into my life.
Lord knows I was not worthy of someone
So excellent, but I collapse within the temple
He has constructed specifically for me.
Her spirit articulates holy instruction,
Pointing towards the neglected staff
Behind our front door. "Prepare the pasture
For plentiful purpose," she says. She wraps
Her mantilla into a scarf around my neck
For warmth and ushers me into the barren tundra
In search of water and fuel to ignite the forest
Within her eyes. I hear the whisper
Of the Lord's promise in her laugh
And see the light of the world shine through her smile
As I make my penitent pilgrimage,
Dancing with the elements. I remind myself
That she carries a radioactive cross cast from lead,
And I must happily carry her across the whirlwind
Of God's favoring decay, pressed persistently
With more precise, pressurizing weight.
Her holy hands calm my malfunctioning mind
And I prostrate myself in prayer at the doorway
To my temple, begging like a stray dog
To be let in out of the rain. She opens the door
To her heart and I return the mantilla to her shoulders
With a steadfast kiss on her forehead.

6:22

You're the most important woman in my life,
The true north pointing the way to peace.
You make me believe in the world.
You remove the film of doubtful cynicism
That veiled my eyes and shattered all hope.
Everything is brighter with you,
Sounds are crisper, emotionally all in.

You plunge me into a pool of imaginative possibilities,
No matter the circumstance, my mind avalanches
Across my consciousness, the hands I hold
To warm my cold palms are yours.
The face I see through the snow is yours.

Our lady stands on my unworthy hands
Until you give permission for me to make
An offering on my beautiful and divine shrine.
The holiest place in the world isn't across the sea
Surrounded by religious and political rigidity.
The holiest place in the world
Is a spring, hidden in the clearing within
The jungle of your eyes.

Somewhere deep in the thicket,
A carpenter is busy at work turning the strongest tree
Into our wedding bed. Into the headboard, he writes
The most important commandment. He waits for us
In the grove, to teach us to shepherd each other
Back to the Lord. I love you with all my heart, my Darling.

Ring

When the final psalm has been sung,
The last stanza has been read,
The closing sermon has been said,
The starting bell will be rung.

For some, it chimes a battle cry,
An explicit call to arms, to take
An extra inch away from the front line.

Others hear the morbid collector's toll,
Piling in as a lump sum payment,
Interest included.

Still more hear an invitation to supper,
Feeding on the sage cautionary wisdom
Of family and friends.

But we hear church bells just over
The horizon, a reminder that a higher
Status of responsibility awaits.

When the final bell has been rung,
The last vow has been read,
The closing prayer has been said,
Our new life together will have begun.

I Love

I love every inch of static energy
Conducting like chain reactive
Explosions over your frontal cortex,
Compelling you to reach out
And place your hand on my face.
I love the steady melody, the beat
That your heart drums across our small
Sheet of the universe. I love treating
Your body like a sanctuary, and finding
Divine reason and connection
When you allow me safe passage
Through the bottomless craters of your soul.
I love the things we create. The worlds
Buried within the depth of your desires,
Begging to be brought up like an ancient
City from the sands—like Atlantis finally
Dug up from the deserts of imagination.
I love the Lord's whisper in my ear when
I look at you. He tells me to be kind
And to earn a higher position in my duty.
I love watching the corrosive reaction
As the particles of time scratch across
Your face with acute precision, now blending
Into tomorrow, rebirthing today, sometime
Until forever becomes yesterday.
I love you.

Sheep

Every night before bed, I tell her to dream of us.
Does she? What grand adventure lies
Just beyond the door of her subconscious?
Secrets so precious, so secure that I shall remain
Forever blind to, groping in the dark for any faint
Glimmer of truth. I long to climb the highest
Mountain within her dreams and conquer
The demons holding pieces of her innocence
Hostage in the pits of her nightmares.
Am I the prince charming in her nocturnal
Fairytales, or am I simply a peasant boy?
Do prophetic apparitions of a life yet to come
Glimmer across her dreams? How many children
Has she counted within the confines of her slumber?
It is only by disciplined accident that we are able
To touch dreams? Caress them we must.
The fruition of our dreams will be like strong and sturdy
Bricks that make up a basilica, dreams designed
To adhere to a higher purpose. One we must wait
Until the night to continue to unfold.

Tears

That is why she cries.
Life is hello and then goodbye.
Left hanging high and dry,
A stolen kiss, a swift black eye.
A drumming rhythm you can't defy.

I will love you till the day I die,
Don't say goodbye. God, no,
Don't cry. Hang on tight,
Better times are nearby.
Please don't cry.

Her Mama once told her
She just wasn't enough.
Blinded by envious pride,
Projecting her own gruff.
But I know her better
So, I'll call her Mama's bluff.
Her daughter is everything,
To me, she's more than enough.

That is why she cries.
Shown love, then she's vilified.
She's left hanging high and dry,
While the others turn a blind eye
And her heart solidifies.

But I love you till the day I die,
Don't grow cold. God, no,
Don't cry. Hang on tight,
Warmer days are nearby.
Please don't cry.

One night I told her,
"I devote my life to you.
It may not be perfect,
But we'll make it through.
I won't stop trying or working,
Even when I don't have a clue.
I'll die trying to prove
Just how much I love you."

That is why she cries.
Consecration till the day I die.
Once alone, now together we arise,
Surveying the potential in the skies.
A surging rhythm we can't defy.

I will love you till the day I die,
There is no goodbye. God, no,
Don't cry. Everything's alright,
I'll always be nearby.
Baby, please don't cry.

Akoya

Pressure, a nucleating process that pries the heart open.
As she makes the first of many delicate incisions,
The stress wrings all moisture from the body, shocks
The systems, and starts signaling a shutdown to the brain.
Fight through the painful temptation to pass out
As she surgically inserts a jagged piece of her bone,
Point first into the folded mantle-like webbing between
The right atrium and the pulmonary artery. The initial pain
Is like a nail dragging its lead feet across a chalkboard sidewalk.
Over time, this irritation will merge with your steady rhythm
And harmonize with the pulsating ripples of the world.

Her bones are now your necessity, but the edges have smoothed
And grafted into an impenetrable lock within your heart.
There is no more pain, and the scars across your chest
Will never fully fade. Thank God for their permanence, too.
Within these lines are written the terms of your ransom
And your reward. But not even you will see the fruits of your labor
Come to prosperous serenity. However, you will feel it. And hear it.
And she'll hear it too. She'll press her ear to your heart
And listen for the faint, slightly offbeat chime. She'll wonder,
What is the color of the growing Akoya that she fertilized
Inside your heart?

Abalone

It took the Lord eight thousand years
To form our relationship,
As if it were part of some
Elaborate, prolonged Easter egg hunt.

First, the Lord cultivated a stubborn shell
And sent a violent tide to sweep it up
Into a current. Our fate circled halfway
Around the world, surrendered to the merciful
Tendencies of the elements,
Before settling off the coast of Coron.
There, it waited. And waited. And waited still.

Then the Lord broke the stone
And gashed the hands of mankind.
As the wound slowly healed,
Understanding washed over His people,
Showering them with gifts
Of technical advancement.
God's people led, herding creatures
And putting a price on societal provision.
Everything was now for sale, including everyone.
Our relationship became valuable,
But nobody knew where to find it, not even us.

Finally, after purposeful actions played out
To a benevolent and malevolent score
As the world turned eight thousand times,
The Lord made us. He freed you and I
To find the relationship
He carefully reserved specifically for us.
We approached our treasure
With the ecstatic joy of a child
Savagely unwrapping a birthday present.

We will have to wait a little longer
Before the Abalone of our friendship
Can be set and fitted into an expression
Of our love. I waited eight thousand years
For the Lord to expose me
To the purest treasure in nature.
I guess I can wait a little longer
Before indulging in our natural serenity.

Melo Melo

She bears a scar upon her heart,
A tear concealed behind her smile.
Blaming herself for being torn apart,
By someone sinister and vile.
He promised her the world to start,
Then left her in a downward spiral.

I'll be there to catch you in the end,
Gathering shattered pieces to mend.
My feelings for you, I can't pretend,
Because above all, you're my friend.

Numb from a broken heart once more,
Another disastrous ending to endure.
This time, she thought she was so smart,
Caught in cycles, she can't comprehend.
Crying in the corner, feeling torn apart,
Can't she find solace God will send?

I will be there to catch you in the end,
Gathering shattered pieces to mend.
My feelings for you, I won't pretend,
Because you're worth it, my dear friend.

Climb out from the darkness, take my hand,
Together, we'll navigate this strange land.
Out of the shadows, take my hand,
Exploring this uncharted strand.
Climb out from the darkness, take my hand,
Building dreams in our own wonderland.

I'll be standing beside you in the end,
Piecing together what needs to be mended.
We're a kaleidoscope, an exciting blend,
Because through it all, you're my best friend.

Biwa

We were united under the watchful eyes of the Lord,
And soon after, my love plucked a golden pearl
From my vaulted heart. I surrendered my treasure
Immediately and without hesitation.

She swallowed the pearl, nestling it deep
Within her stomach. Already priceless, its worth
Grew with each passing day. Eve's scriptural promise
Wrapped my wife in a cocoon of steadfast devotion.

As her body faltered, I wrestled with anxious desire.
The weight of our treasure burdened us both,
Teaching me the art of giving everything
While leaving the scraps for myself.

We both knew this golden pearl wasn't truly ours,
A day will come when we offer it, a symbol of devotion,
Among our treasures. Each pearl, a testament
To love tenderly and without end.

Manifesting

In a dream, Our Gentle Lady appeared to me,
Calling my name with a smile of grace.
I rose to her, tears of joy streaming,
"Have I done well, Most Reverent?" I asked.

She unveiled herself, placing her mantilla in my hands,
A shooting star streaking through the mirrored cosmos,
I cradled planets colliding in vibrant chaos,
Kaleidoscopic swirls of stardust
Embraced by gravitational wombs, to be reborn.

"Go, my child," she whispered, lifting my gaze
To behold God's promise in her hazel eyes.
"I grant universal protection to the one you crown
With heavens' embrace. These events woven in cloth
Are vast and powerful, some may test your faith,
But fear not, my son, they are carefully stitched."

"Go to her, wrap her in my loving promise,
So, she and your children may one day know
The tender mercy of the Lord."

A Wound

The timber bled green, sap flowing freely,
As we made our first defiant incision.
At the edge of the glen where she
Fed me water honeyed with her tears,
Extracted the arrowhead that nearly
Pierced my heart and etched our love story
Upon nature's immutable parchment. No court
Would heed our plea for reason, our houses
Stood in opposition. Our kiss a sin defiant of decree.

To consort with the enemy meant death,
Yet we defied our courts and accepted the consequences.
In times of war and peace, we persist,
Chased each other across faded horizons.
As long as timber bleeds against
The elements' fury, we linger,
Whispering gently and cursing cacophonously
On tongues of those who question,
"Who were these heart-struck rogues?"

Pearl of my Heart

What if I told you we've met before?
Long before love crossed our minds.

Not in this lifetime, but through countless others,
Each time remembering more faint glimmers.

Like waking from a deep slumber,
Briefly capturing memories before they fade.

In each rebirth, God sets us on a quest
To seek each other out and say yes.

Sometimes, I found you crippled by fear,
Haunted by past men's broken vows.

Other times, your light shone brightest,
Our lips meeting in pure fulfillment.

In one life, you rescued me from drowning,
Lost in the depths of a half-empty bottle.

In another, you lacked for nothing,
Every desire fulfilled with ease.

What is time to souls whose destiny
Was written by celestial hands?

We were always meant to fall in love,
Outside time, every time as if anew.

God sent me on a journey to find
The pearl of my heart.

I returned to his altar
Holding gently onto your hand.

Worthy

Once, a fair maiden bathed at the edge
Of a waterfall after a long ride through the countryside.
Above, celestial creatures gathered,
Captivated by her unchallenged beauty.
Each drop that kissed her skin turned holy,
Ignited by the spiritual fire within her unblemished soul.
One by one, cherubim threw themselves at her feet,
Offering wings and halos for a day of matrimony.
For a human to kiss an angel meant excommunication,
A sentence of death for the celestial being.
Unafraid, she declined each flattering bid,
Resolute in honoring the second commandment.
Deflated, the cherubs retreated, cautious not to ignite
Fire in the maiden's eyes, returning orderly to the Shepherd's fold
—save one.

One angel begged permission to stay, to watch over
God's beloved pearl, granted on the condition:
Do not fall in love with her; her heart belongs to a man.
Agreed, the angel kept watch through thirty joyous moons,
As the maiden returned often to purify herself at the falls.

One fateful day, marauders passed through her land,
With lustful, evil intentions in their hearts.
The heavenly protector, bound by oath,
Watched in terror as they stalked their unsuspecting prey.
Unable to interfere, the angel's heart broke,
Imagining a savage outcome.

Moments before the attack, the cherub unsheathed his dagger,
Seared his chest with a cut, and careened into the void.
As the blade struck the ground, the earth shook violently,
Alerting the maiden and scattering the thieves in shameful retreat.

Finding the angel mortally wounded, all that remained—
A lone feather from his wing. Weeping, she clutched the relic,
Terrified God's immortal wind might catch hold.

Meanwhile, a knight of high rank, shaken by the quake,
Came upon her, offering aid and captivated by her gaze.
Smiling, she accepted his escort back to the kingdom,
Where he hoisted her onto his horse and rode vigilantly home.

Keshi

At the edge of the waterfall, with nowhere to go but down,
We faced the relentless pursuit of ravenous wolves.
Their hunger matched our frantic heartbeat,
Echoing in the cacophony of the rushing water.
Locked onto our elevated rhythm, they hurdled into the current,
Chomping covetously at the icy spray.

Your mortal stare seared my eyes,
Trembling fingernails drew blood from my skin,
Invigorating the furious wolves with the scent of fear.
Options dwindled by the millisecond,
Death's voice hidden under the breath of the wind,
Its shadow closing in from all sides.

But in that perilous moment,
Amidst the chaos and impending doom,
All I heard was her cries.
I kissed her tear-streaked face,
Pulled her into an unbreakable embrace,
Whispered "I love you" as if it were our last
And defied the wind's harsh instructions.

Together, we plunged into the abyss,
Surrendering to the Lord's final judgment.
Silence engulfed us devastatingly,
As our bodies cleaved the surface like a knife.
In the watery cocoon, we held each other,
Breathless, suspended in time.

Then, God's merciful hand plunged into the depths,
Rescuing us from the freezing tomb.
A lone wolf, driven by desperation,
Had leaped after us, only to meet its demise on sharp rocks.
We swam to shore, heartbeats echoing relief,
Gasping on the sweet flavor of sky and freedom,

I cradled my wife's face against my chest,
Offering thanks for God's intervening love,
Which spared us from the jaws of death,
And reaffirmed our trust in each other,
In the enduring power of love.

Mystery of Love

The word of God descends upon the world like rainwater,
Softly touching the body of a stagnant lake.
Messages drum a steady beat upon its surface,
Rippling out disciplined instructions.

Each tender drop of water meeting water beats a song,
Echoing the sounds a child hears resting on his mother's chest,
Harmonizing with the gentle murmur against a lover's breast,
And softly fading as a daughter weeps into her father's heart.

God's majestic symphonies traverse the universal human heart,
Like a formidable hurricane, their artistic direction lost
In the wild, untamed music of the storm.
Yet in the eye, amidst the chaos, there is peace.

To decipher the eternal message, to heed the counsel against fear,
One must stand resolute in the eye of the storm.
Sometimes, raindrops upon the pool fall silently,
Until God breaks a branch to make a louder splash.

Study the place where the tree surrendered its limb,
Beneath the wound, find a heart embracing two eternal letters,
Chiseled forever across the bark.

Blister

A lamb, astray from its flock, stumbled into a treacherous mud pit,
Struggling in vain against its grip, marring its snow-white wool.
With each desperate kick, it sank deeper, cries of distress echoing
As the sun descended toward the horizon.

The pitiful bleats caught the attention of a cunning fox nearby,
Its hunger roused by the vulnerable lamb. Stealthily, it stalked,
Concealed among the brush, eyeing its prey with focused intent.
But in the stillness, it failed to detect the approaching shepherd.

Silent as a shadow, the shepherd advanced, keenly aware of the danger,
Brandishing a heavy staff with practiced skills. Swift and resolute,
He struck the surprised fox, its plans thwarted as it tried to retaliate.
Yet the shepherd's blows were relentless, driving the fox to retreat.

With the immediate threat subdued, the shepherd turned to the lamb,
Wasting no time in rescuing it from the clinging mud's embrace.
His gentle hands lifted the trembling creature, soothing its fear,
Cradling it against his chest, a protective barrier against harm.

Through the field they moved, the shepherd and his precious charge,
Returning to the safety of the flock and the familiar pastures.
With compassion in his voice, the shepherd reassured the lamb,
Guiding it to peace and safety, away from the trials of the day.

Faceted

Let's embark on a bike ride,
I've room aplenty for two,
You perched on my handlebars,
I'll pedal, guiding us through.
Wind tousles your hair,
Dark brown in its hue,
Pedaling fast, we soar,
Above skies of deep blue.

Surprise seizes me,
When you kiss with such grace,
I gaze into your eyes,
Finding solace and place.
Your love, a melody,
A harmonious embrace,
Long-awaited and cherished,
In your arms, I find peace.

In mass, hold my hand tight,
Spiritual battles wage war,
Prayers for reconciliation,
Heart raw to its core.
Unpacking the past's weight
Cannot evade anymore,
Your presence brings solace,
A goal worth striving for.

Surprise envelops me,
In each tender kiss we share,
Heaven's glimpse in your eyes,
I plunge into their care.
Our love, a symphony,

Harmonious and rare,
The world may falter around,
But together, we dare.

Conch

Angels descended from heaven's height,
Their kiss upon our foreheads, a blessing bright,
Father's nod sanctified our bond that day,
Though spring's chill gripped, our hearts ablaze.

Even the sun peeked through clouds' veil,
To witness our union, our souls unveil,
Beneath the shepherd's tender gaze,
"God be with you, my children," he praised.

His words, carried by the whispering wind,
Blessing like perfumed oils, they've pinned,
To our hair, our skin, anointing divine,
Marking us as one in heavenly design.

In that moment, my spirit danced free,
In gardens of old, beneath wisdom's tree,
Tasting nectar of blossoms, life's sweet sip,
Echoing her lips, the taste on mine's tip.

Returning to the world's ordered beat,
Sign of our Lord, in reverence complete,
Father's voice bid us, "Go in peace,"
Hand in hand, our journey to increase.

Together, ready to face the world's test,
Bound by love, by God's grace, blessed.

In the Meantime

The dimpled indent,
Above her smile's corner,
Is simply captivating.

Nations would sway,
To hear the feather
That tickles her laughter.

The world could ignite,
By the candle's end
That warms her.

Fortunes lost,
Decades spent,
Empires crumbled,
For her favor.

Many offer everything,
I have so little.

So, wring me dry,
Extract my last
Drop of desire.

With faith,
like a mustard seed,
Mountains bow.

Imagine, with just a molecule
Of commitment,
What we could achieve.

Tahitian

We thought we understood passion,
But the heat from our fire paled
In comparison to the one that took
The plot. The plants. The house.
Everything kissed by the fire.

We knew nothing about passion.
Collecting fragmented pieces
Of our past as we sifted through
The soot. Each treasure found
Was an additional mockery.

Hitting the bottom of this trench
Hurt like a brick to the cheek.
She was devastated after the fire.
We put the pieces we could salvage
In a shoebox and spent the night
Wrapped in each other's arms.

The following day, we gathered
The metal, and sold it for pennies
On the dollar. We constructed
The remaining scrap into a
Patchwork roof so that we
May be spared from the rain.

Destruction is expensive
But we vowed not to put a price
On our honor. We learned to be
As dangerously patient as owls.
We hardly look at each other.
Now we stand back-to-back,
Constantly on alerted guard.

The night we watched the fire
Take everything, I fed it my vice.
I knew she would watch what I do,
And adopt my ritualistic habits.
Most of our free time is now spent
In prayerful thanksgiving. That despite
The loss, at least we have each other.

Light is Born

The hands in our hands
Are no longer our hands.
These hands are small,
Hands we clutch onto
Tighter than each other's hands,
Terrified these hands will slip
Right through our fingers.

These hands are like saplings,
And one day, we will no longer
Be able to wrap our hands
Fully embracing the trunk.
Their hands will outstretch
Our reach, and grasp at the light.
Their limbs no longer yield
To the touch of our hands.

These small hands are doomed
To outgrow the strength,
The work of our very own hands.
Our hands raisin and fray
Like a tomato left in the sun.
Even then, our hands will reach
Out to clutch onto the promise
Of small sapling-like hands.

Taking Wing

Do you believe in forever?
Do you trust in God?
Does He pair us together?
Or is it just a facade?

Pearls and diamonds
Bespeckle the floor.
Royal purple hydrangeas
Woven into the door.
And a woman in white
Who's ready to soar.

Will our bond last forever?
Were we ordained by God?
Side by side, we walk together
Tearing down the facade.

A covenant hidden
In a binding kiss.
Eyes closed,
Bodies in bliss.
Reborn, rising
From the abyss.

We believe in forever,
Treading the path of God.
We were meant to last forever.
To infinity and beyond.

Permission

Come on in and sit down, boy.
Tell me, what's on your mind,
Boy. What do you want?
You're a dangerous détente,
Boy. A beautiful mistaken mess,
But you're learning and fighting on,
Boy. Are you ready for this,
Do you know what it means, boy?
Are you firm on the ground,
Or floating 'round in a dream,
Boy? You need to level with me.
30 years forward. 30 years back.
What do you see, boy? Time flies
By rather quickly. You better
Be good to her, honest and loyal,
Treat her like she's royal, boy.
You must sacrifice everything
And abandon the boy
To know fulfillment and joy.
Best of luck and godspeed,
My boy.

A promise

She feels like she's the only one
Who's trusted falling before.
Maybe she'll splat the ground,
But he knows that she'll soar.

See just how she flies
Above the skies.
Sparks in her eyes,
Having won the prize.

Heavenly stardust guides her way
Across blue skies that were once gray,
And deep in her heart is a girl at play.
Flying like a bird, wasting the day.

Blessed love crystallized
Better than she fantasized,
In a sweet compromise
Till the day that he dies.

Two Sapphires

Our Lady lays her hand
On the girl's shoulder
And whispers, "You are loved,"
As Our Lady slips the sparkling
Promise down the girl's finger.
It fits finer than a silk glove,
Our Lady smiles as it winks,
Dances hues of crisp water
Blue in the light radiating,
Peeking from behind Our Lady.
Tears pour like water from shale
Out of the girl's eyes. Forgiveness
Glints at the corner of Our Lady's
Smile. "Go to him," she says,
Pointing to the man struggling
With a cumbersome plow
In the distant field.
"His cross is heavy.
He cannot lift it on his own."

2:20

We walked through the valley of fossilized titans
In search of the fountain of youth. Long ago,
These colossal beasts nearly leveled the mesa
As they warred over the drink. Now, all that remains
Are dried-out husks, like a bowl of vibrant fruit
Left to dehydrate in a wooden sauna. The heat
Can mislead the hazy mind and the pungent odors
Of aspen sage stains the fingertips like tobacco.

We scaled the ancient imprints of violent collisions
Against the landscape, particles of fossilized bone
Nestling within the webbings of our feet as we struggled
To find footholds. The twists and jagged edges
Of the stone seem to enclose around us like hands
Catching a dragonfly. What mercy would these giant beasts
Have shown long ago if they beheld two mortals trespassing
On their land? Would they enclose their hands around us?

Shadows sprinted against the sun, and when all hope
Seemed lost, we spotted the gentle reflection of the oasis
At the bowl of the Northern Gate. Ecstasy ripped at our clothes
As we ran towards the pool, and the waters caressed us
When we broke the glass-like surface. The waters
Poured down our throats like honey and settled
With a warm thud in our guts. The youthful joy in her eyes
Sparkled like a diamond as they locked the moment in time.

Acorns Falling

Called to consumption
But I choose to create
The acorns are coming
You can't count 'em
There's no time to wait
Just trust and fall through
The water feels great
Life's blessings, a blanket
Surrender, there's no escape
Keep breathing
Keep breathing – Ouch
Falling acorns shake me to shape

Enough

Let's go for a long walk,
On an adventure overdue
Let's get lost in the forest,
We've got nothing else to do.
Let's run away together,
I wanna fall in love with you.
Let's build our own empire,
Making all our dreams come true.

Let's go for a swim
And dive in the ocean blue.
Let's dig for black pearls
In a world we never knew.
Let's catch the biggest tuna
And throw a feast for two.
Let's cultivate God's talents
And make all our dreams come true.

Let's go for a picnic,
Bring a basket of bamboo.
Let's lay in the sunlight,
I feel at peace with you.
Let's spend our lives together
And see the seasons through.
Let's get married on Sunday,
My answer is "I do".

Golden

By Kitch

He looked at me as though,
I'm the only woman in the room.
Hazel brown eyes, wrapping
A swirl of evergreen forest.

Crowded room, loud and full of laughter,
But my laughter ceased when he looked
At me lovingly with a question
That elevated my anxiety.

"Do you want to dance with me?"

Clumsy on my feet,
He guided me through the dance floor
With such ease
That I started to trust myself with him.

Eyes full of love,
I brought down the last
Reserve of my walls,
Letting his love flow through.

Golden as the dress that I possessed,
Lighting up the dark world I lived in.
His love is the light that would guide
Me through salvation, surrendering myself
To his love and to the love
We will have as one in the future.

Special Thanks

*T*o my Mother and Father and every couple who taught me how to love with honor and care. Your powerful example reminds me to stay grounded in my devotion toward a higher purpose and to attend to the chores of love with joyful resolve.

To James Dodson, Mark Delgado, and Charles Mitchell. Thank you for inspiring me to strive in the direction of matrimony. You helped me understand what it means to be my own man and the traits I should look for in a potential mate. I hope my future family will one day inspire yours with the same profound impact (and more) that you have had on my life.

To my family, love is difficult and can bring out the best and worst in each member of a loving family. Thank you for the patience you've shown when I've sunk to my worst and for your support when I've shined at my brightest.

To Kitch. I never thought I would ever meet a woman as excellent as you are. Without you, I was resigned to being a mediocre version of myself. But with you, I take careful, proactive daily steps to become the best possible version of myself. Thank you for saying yes. For jumping into my arms. For walking eye to eye and side by side.

About the Author

Vitale is excited to release his second collection of poetry. He self-published his first work, *Life Chosen*, on November 4th, 2022. *Life Chosen* is an introspective look into the spiritual journey of a modern Catholic struggling to find his place in the Lord's pasture. Vitale originally planned to follow up his first collection with a deeper dive into the spiritual world, but the Lord had other ideas. Vitale met a woman, and with newfound inspiration from his girlfriend (fiancée as of publication), he shifted the theme of his second collection to a different focus.

Vitale was born near Pavlodar, Kazakhstan and grew up in the Dominion suburbs outside of Washington D.C., where he currently lives and works in finance. Vitale received a BA in Theatre with a minor in Poetry. He started writing poetry at Bishop O'Connell High School under the guidance of his creative writing teacher, Tom Duesterhaus. Tom introduced Vitale to authors like Milton, Keats, Emerson, Tappan, Akhmatova, etc., and encouraged his young students to submit original poems to the yearly school journal of creative works.

Because this is Vitale's second collection, he still feels as though he is only starting to refine his craft and scratch the surface in understanding the deeper meanings behind universal workings. Vitale is blessed by the overwhelming gifts the Lord has laid at his feet, and hopes God continues to stoke the creative fire in his heart.

Made in the USA
Columbia, SC
08 November 2024